Benching With Virgil

Gad Hollander

Pivotal Prose Series

Avec Books

Also by Gad Hollander:

The smallness of it all
Page
Video Residua (Orphic)
Figures of Speech
Sleep, Memory
The Palaver (with images by Andrew Bick)
Walserian Waltzes

FILMS/VIDEOS:
Mnemosyne
Background Music (Orphic)
Euripides' Movies
Diary of a Sane Man
The Palaver Transcription

AUDIO:
The Palaver (CD)

Benching With Virgil

ISBN:1-880713-24-1

Library of Congress Control Number: 00-134461

Cover photograph by Gad Hollander

Cover design by Colleen Barclay

First Edition

The Pivotal Prose Series
is an imprint of Avec Books
P.O. Box 1059
Penngrove, CA 94951

bensh, tr. and intr. v., to bless; to say grace–
Yiddish *benschen,* fr. dial. OF. *bencheir* (OF.
beneir, F. *bénir*), fr. L. *Benedicere.*
—*KLEIN'S ETYMOLOGICAL DICTIONARY OF THE
ENGLISH LANGUAGE*

THE ARGUMENT

ONE VISITS GREAT cities. But it is not necessarily there that one happens on her for the first time. It appears, however, that this is indeed a great city, in reputation as in size, and that she, seated quite erect in the middle of an unornamented bench, has chosen this small, insignificant park, or square, the way a scrupulous scholar might select an unobtrusive niche amidst the ranks of books in a library. All the more commendable her choice when one considers how this city bends and sprawls in every direction, laying down temptations of all kinds in one's path. Alternatively, as suggested, one may come across her in a small provincial town, or a quaint village, where a modest park or square....

*

She is seated quite erect, propping a book on her lap, her hands cupped loosely round its binding, its spine half-sunk, limply but naturally, in the trough of her skirt, between her thighs.

*

Despite the outdoors, which are airy and unpredictable, the leaves do not flutter. Her pink thumbs hook round them on either side, without protruding from the margins onto the text. One supposes the right-hand margins are broader and more uneven than the left-hand ones, which are always flush. The right-hand thumb, whilst remaining wary of the unpredictable fluctuations in the width of the margin, is allowed considerable free play. In contrast, the left-hand side's attendant thumb must rivet itself to a permanent position on the margin, identical on every page, lest it impinge on the text and thereby possibly obscure a meaning. One is led to believe, however, that this constancy has a reassuring effect on her.

*

A lack of familiarity with the topography of the region causes some concern about the light's immediate prospects. One is vaguely certain as to its source, but whether that source is advancing or receding cannot be ascertained as yet. At the worst, there is some time left before it dies completely. Within such a theoretical time span one's predictions might, with equal facility, be confirmed or contradicted. The light illumines the right side of her body, its source suspended not more than ten or fifteen degrees off the uneven horizon of the skyline. One cannot be more precise.

*

A tress or lock of hair does not curve or flow over either shoulder. Her head is tilted towards the open book, at a slight angle with the axis of her backbone and a little to one side, her right. Her hair is not golden, though the light lends it a bias of that hue. Her eyelids conceal her eyes, and but for the appendage of eyelashes would make one think of the eyes of ancient statues, as indeed her entire body would make one think of a statue. Intermittently, however, her right hand completely loosens its already loose grip on the book. Half the book is momentarily supported solely by her lap and left palm. In an exact and flowing movement, her middle finger alights on the upper (nearest, from here) right-hand corner of the page, whilst her thumb, an inch or two nearer the lower part of her torso, rests lightly on the edge of the page, at the extremity of the margin. The movement remains uninterrupted as the middle finger, with a gentle thrust in the thumb's direction, carefully bends the corner of the leaf into a wavelet, then slides beneath it as the leaf springs back to its original plane shape. Immediately the thumb lifts from the page and, with the aid of one or two of her other fingers, steered by her wrist and forearm, the leaf is delicately pushed to the left, inscribing an imaginary arc as it falls into place on the left-hand side. Simultaneous with the leaf's fall, the attendant thumb on the left is worked free of its position, while the right hand follows and smoothes down the leaf before the left-hand thumb resumes an almost identical position on the verso of the new page. As if to remove any extraneous matter that may have collected in the turning, the right hand, in a single upward stroke, brushes the page once before sweeping back across the unread text. It, too, resumes its old position: thumb hooked over the margin, fingers splayed along the binding. The head has not moved.

*

The knees, protruding from the upper rim of skirt, do not touch. Beyond their rime, a deepening shadow. One imagines an obscure crevasse, perhaps just below the book's spine. One has two alternatives: to squat or to stand, as if one's feet were rooted among a million grassblades; or worse, as if entombed in a concrete slab, as in a Laurel & Hardy movie. One recalls clandestine criminal elements lurking in the night in such movies.

*

Her indeterminate moods are not given to subjective interpretation. The book shuts. The left hand has brought half the binding round in a semi-circle. Consequently, the spine has been lifted slightly from the trough of her skirt and now faces the expanse of park and city to her left. The thumbs have been casually extricated from their positions on the margins and now rest without purpose on the hard surface of the cover. She lifts her head a little but her eyes remain lowered, almost shut, as if reflecting on the text. One cannot determine her mood, even less the matter of her thoughts. Perhaps that is only natural. For if one were able to share in her contemplation one might conceivably detect her thoughts, or the objects contemplated, by way of her mood. Perhaps, if one's eyes were also lowered, or shut.... But they are not. For the moment she is motionless, but for the shallow undulations of her breathing torso.

It was in January, if I remember. The curtains were already drawn by late afternoon. She lies motionless, face down on the floor, her legs spread across the little hearth-rug by the bed. The lamp on one of the sidetables is overturned and rests on its shade. Its light shines on her hair and part of her back. A hazy line of shadow runs obliquely over her middle- and lower-back. The lower part of her body is completely submerged in that dimmer, more diffuse light. A book is strewn in the middle of the room, near the foot of the bed, where the light is considerably weaker, a darksome light. She may have been reading it earlier that afternoon, or it may have fallen from the table near the centre of the room. In any case, it lies on its spine with the pages fanned open. If she has been reading it, it is impossible to say at what page she stopped or, indeed, whether she has even started it or, perhaps, finished it.

We enter the room through a doorway on the right connecting with an adjacent room. Mr Laurel is seated behind the desk, set in the recess of the bay window. The curtains are drawn. Near the centre of the room stands a low rectangular table; on the table, a book. Judging from its thickness it may be a novel or a history book, or perhaps the complete works of a poet. It looks like a new edition, with the dust-jacket still intact, and is probably as yet unread. To the left of the table, between two identical sidetables supporting identical lamps, stands the bed, its large mahogany head-board pressed against the wall. At the far end of the room, equidistant from the centre table and the desk and facing the latter at an angle, stands a chaise-longue on which Bergson is comfortably perched. His left arm lies lengthways along the back of the sofa, while his right arm hangs loosely over the side facing the room. He seems to be twirling a greyish-green viscid pellet with the thumb and forefinger of his right hand. He has been listening attentively, while exploring his nostrils, to Mr Laurel expounding on the desperate loneliness of the writer's profession, particularly the poet's. Mr Laurel has said that it is an incomparably solitary profession and has offered some concrete examples as evidence for his statement. He has argued that, unlike actors, musicians, painters and the like, the writer – especially the poet – has no public forum in which to exhibit his stuff. Bergson has nodded in agreement. And Mr Laurel has gone even further and maintained that whereas a playwright will view the fruits of his labours through the medium of the stage, and the novelist, if successful, will see his book skilfully transformed into moving (and talking) pictures, or at least prominently displayed in bookshop windows all over the city, the poet, alas, however praiseworthy his song, is at the best of times doomed to obscurity: his work, even when published, is tucked narrowly away among the back shelves of a few select bookshops. Mr Laurel has emphasised 'select'. If he has any readers, they are mostly fellow practitioners who are more often envious than appreciative of his work. Isn't it a crying shame, Mr Laurel has asked rhetorically, especially when the exact opposite of the situation had once been the norm. Wasn't it so in antiquity? For his part, Bergson has said very little except that poets are still held in high esteem, if only by a few. At another point he has added, this should not, nor does it, detract from their merits; on the contrary, it only serves to elevate their song to an almost sublime pitch, and what would the philistines do with such music but drown it in their own cacophony? Bergson has retorted with his own rhetorical question. Mr Laurel is on the verge of tears, but restrains himself. Since L's disappearance and the subsequent discovery of her body, he suspects Bergson of complicity – but with whom and in what sort of scheme he is as yet unsure. Bergson lights a cigarette and changes the topic as we enter the room. Nasty business, he says. Through the open doorway the shifting of table and chairs can be heard. Presumably Mr Hardy is hanging up the lace curtains which he has recently laundered. He hums a light tune to himself as he works. The door, however, shuts behind us, cutting off Mr Hardy's air. In the room the sole source of light is the lamp on Mr Laurel's desk.

Coincidental with the narrator's dream is the reader's (qua reader) disappearance from one's mind, as though that figure occupied a previous, now fading dream. He is watching television with L. In moderate, digestible doses, the programme depicts life in a death camp. A dramatised documentary. Narrator and L, before as well as after the show, discuss its ethical and aesthetic implications, argue its validity within their current historical context, refer to other sources, in small, reserved voices, as in a gallery, before and after, in front of the glazy olive screen, cooling, or about to be warmed. They eat and drink nothing during the hour of its airing. The narrator smokes several cigarettes; L is a non-smoker. A scene recounts the death of a man for whom escape and suicide have become synonymous. The action seems well rehearsed: from an overview shot of some twenty or thirty men laboriously wielding their implements inside a vast, half-dug, rectangular pit, the camera cuts to a medium shot of a figure who has just dropped his pickaxe and whose face (in close-up), despite a wry, jocular appearance, bears traces of tears among its pock-marks and bristles. After an initial hesitation, the actor scrambles up the slope of the pit towards the left of the screen (the camera following him from a fixed position) then, on reaching level ground, breaks into a lame trot and heads for the fence which looms in the background. In following him, the camera has glimpsed one or two dumb, inoffensive gazes from the crowd of prisoners. Before he reaches the fence a whistle is heard, followed immediately by a shouted command, then a second whistle followed by a sarcastic warning shot. The man has only a few more feet to run, a diminishing figure in the centre of the screen, before he latches onto the electrified fence with a muffled scream. Cut, simultaneous with second shouted command, to watchtower. As more whistles and commands are heard the images begin to melt away, taking with them the screen itself, the companion, the furniture and cigarette smoke, until the whole room is momentarily enveloped in darkness, yet only momentarily, for then the images reform, slowly, crystallising with acrid urgency, with a poignancy too true-to-life, with characters whose likeness is almost perfect, and with a smell that hangs close but cannot be described. Familiar with the literature, the visitant draws comfort from his knowledge. For as far as he can remember, he does not figure in any of the chronicles, neither directly nor indirectly nor in any symbolic or metaphorical way. Yet, as if by some primal instinct, his behaviour immediately complies with these demonic circumstances. He shuffles aimlessly among the condemned. He obeys orders. To the best of his abilities he establishes routines in his daily existence in order to maintain his moral strength. But these are only gestures, he knows. He knows that for the executioner death is merely a formality, a tedious bureaucratic stamp, a means towards an idea. Nevertheless, he feels his knowledge to be a kind of hindsight – perhaps he has dreamt this or is dreaming it now – and his presence a kind of absence, an invisible presence. At times he believes he will pass through it all unscathed, like an insect through a combine harvester. He knows that others have, somehow;

he has read their testimony. But theirs was a twofold struggle against death and sleep, whereas for him sleep and death have become synonymous, something to be succumbed to at the end of the day.

Upon waking the narrator returns to the scene of the crime, where L has reappeared. Reappeared, that is, from his own point of view. She seems to have acquired supernatural, or at least unnatural, qualities in her absence. She is walking on a cushion of air about three inches above the ground and her body is infused with light, a light inseparable from the light in the room, without a visible source. She takes a few steps towards the centre of the room and stops. The light is such that it neither passes through her, as through glass, nor reflects off her, as off any opaque material (say, a wall). Nor does it emanate from within her own body. Yet while all the other objects in the room seem to have shadows coupled to their parts that extend from their variously shaped edges and crooks – albeit in a curiously inconsistent manner: the shadow of the centre table, for instance, the table-top properly speaking, extends towards the bed, whereas the shadows of its legs cast themselves in four parallel lines in the opposite direction, namely the direction of the desk, whose shadow in turn runs towards, and overlaps with, the shadow of Bergson's chaise-longue; moreover, Bergson's own shadow falls behind him, namely behind the sofa's end-rest, running obliquely on the floor in the direction of the room's western wall – while these objects, then, at least have some form of shadow, she, and every part of her anatomy, casts no shadow whatsoever: neither under her chin nor under her nose, nor inside her nostrils, nor along their outer base, nor directly under her lower lip, nor under her eyes or her eyebrows, nor under her breasts or between her thighs or along the inside of her calves, nor under her ankles or anywhere along the floor under her naked feet, nor anywhere her arms might cast a shadow while gesturing or, not gesturing, hanging loosely at her sides. Only a soft radiance everywhere, neither brighter nor dimmer than the light in the room, nor indeed separable from it, as has already been mentioned. The narrator finds himself at a loss for words, while Bergson is discussing with Mr Laurel the possible motives for her murder. The others, of which there are few, though unknown and unnamed, are talking amongst themselves as well, but the topics of their several conversations, not to mention the actual substance of their dialogues, remain incomprehensible, for the only audible words or phrases are of a neutral and almost meaningless kind: she, and, it looks, who, they, as if, as, whether, then he, so, said. The syllables weave in and out of Bergson's and Mr Laurel's conversation like street sounds, but it appears that neither has taken any notice of them. Bergson has been suggesting revenge. To which Mr Laurel has given a silent but reserved nod, qualified with a raising of his eyebrows, a slight drooping of the corners of his mouth, and a barely perceptible shrug of the shoulders.

Virgil was living in Paris at the time, whither the young writer went to read him a chapter from his book. If he would want to hear more the writer would readily and gratefully oblige, for he would interpret the poet's tolerance first as a sign of forgiveness for his audacious behaviour in calling upon him on the off-chance, without proper notice, and secondly as implicit praise for the work in question. If the poet would want to hear more.... But would he want to hear anything at all? Would he even exchange greetings with him? There was no question of that, at least not for the moment. For the moment he would read the chapter and Virgil would listen attentively. And praise it? Ah! That, he thought, was the dubious calling card perched neatly on a tray, held breast-high by an anonymous butler and brought in to the poet, brought out, returned, no, not returned, replied ... at any rate a card culled from an image in one of his poems, irrefutably present to poet and reader alike. That, he thought, as he left his flat and caught the bus to Victoria, as he boarded the train at Victoria and alighted at Dover, as he embarked at Dover and disembarked at Calais, as he boarded the Paris train at Calais and alighted from it at the Gare du Nord, and as he got on and as he got off innumerable buses – for Paris was a strange city and he was wont to lose his way in strange cities; and in the drawn-out intervals as well, that is, between embarkations and disembarkations, as he sat on the upper deck between Mornington Crescent and Victoria Station and through the misty window waved good-bye with his mind's hand to the people, cars, machinery and landmarks that constituted the city, or as he sat on the train between Victoria and Dover, or as he sat on the ferry – where he also stood up and ambulated from time to time, as is the custom on ships, even ferries – between Dover and Calais, or as he sat on the Paris-bound train not speaking to his fellow passengers (of whom there were three, a family, in his compartment), for he was timid and, besides, did not speak French, or as, later, he sat in the Metro briefly, giving up his seat with a dumb gesture to a wounded war veteran whose left leg was amputated above the knee, as was the right, though the former was longer than the latter, and who may not have been a war veteran after all – though how was he to know – but a victim of a post-war (or pre-war for that matter, for the man was elderly to boot) traffic accident, or both, that is to say a war veteran in one leg and a traffic accident victim in the other, though which leg was lost in what circumstances was impossible to determine without accosting the man and exchanging long and detailed biographical anecdotes, which neither did, the one because he was timid and did not speak the language (as already stated) and the other because he got off the train only two stops after getting on, the seat quickly being snatched up by a determined looking spinster (or widow) in her early sixties whose intentions the writer had not noticed until it was too late, for he was too busy deciphering the name of the station when this exchange took place while at the same time pondering with deep thoughts the cause of the unfortunate amputee's loss of limb, whether both legs had been lost simultaneously, that is as a result of only one accident or land-mine or mortar shell, or whether only one, say the left, which was after all longer, was lost originally, say in the war, while the other, the right, was lost in the post-war period, say in a traffic accident, which might account for their varying lengths, or whether the left was the one lost in a traffic accident and the right the one lost in the war, or whether both had been lost in the war or both in a traffic accident, or whether the left in a post-war traffic accident and the right in a pre-war traffic accident, the poor man consequently being embarrassingly mistaken for a war hero during and after the war, or whether any of those given permutations was in fact vice versa, or as, after leaving the Metro, he sat or stood in one or more of the innumerable buses – which (his standing or sitting) depended on the direction the buses were taking and the time of day – if, for example, he was on a bus between the hours of 7a.m. and 8a.m. or 3p.m. and 4p.m. heading towards the city centre, or between 1p.m. and 2p.m. or 7p.m. and 8p.m. heading away from the city centre, he would most likely have been standing, but if he was on a bus at the same times but heading in the opposite directions, or heading in the same directions but at the alternative times, he would most likely have been sitting, but if, however, he was on a bus at any other time but between 7a.m. and 8a.m. or 1p.m. or 2p.m. or between 3p.m. and 4p.m. or 7p.m. and 8p.m. and heading either towards or away from the city centre, or neither towards nor away from, but around the city centre, then he would most likely have been free to choose whether to sit or to stand, and his choice would most likely have depended upon the length of his journey, that is to say, he would most likely have been standing for a short journey and sitting for a longer one, which is quite natural – so as he sat or stood on one or more of innumerable buses, only one of which bore him towards his ultimate destination, his being timid and ignorant of the language (as already stated, several times) making him prone to losing his way, that, together with a few intervening thoughts, phrases and images, preoccupied his mind more than anything else that day. Or, rather, that and another equally weighty idea which had become a nagging nightmare of his waking life. It plagued him whenever the idea of praise subsided into some sort of rational perspective, or, to put it bluntly, whenever he vied with boredom. And the idea was simply that a writer writes, that he needs neither praise nor censure, that his craft requires diligence and care, that his art demands a loyal heart (artistically speaking), that writing is life and life is writing and that he for whom the two are separable is not a writer but a scribbler-by-numbers, a player-pianist, a Zeno of Xerox, a rune-running penmanship pimp, or, as in the case of some or most best-selling authors, a prodigiously prolix pimple – in short, a prick with a nib, a nebbish with a pen; and what was more, to write was to obey a command, to practise a commandment, and the command was to write, and the commandment was also to write, just like that, in the infinitive of all moods, not, as would be expected, the imperative, which did not deter him but, on the contrary, roused him to write, and to write again, to obey and to write, and sometimes, when he discerned the equivocal nature of the commandment and the ambiguous tone of the command, not to write, for to write was, in a sense, not to write, just as to live was, in a sense, not to live; still, to write and not to write, that was the imperative given to him, the action demanded, with which he complied at all times, for at all times, as it happened, he was either writing or not writing. Why then, one may well ask, did he persist with his fetish for praise? The answer, one supposes, follows.

The writer said: They drift in, they drift out, being at times ideas, at times characters, at other times ideas about characters, at other times still characterisations of ideas.

Then some of the characters spoke.

The reader said: If I fell would I break anything? Any bones, I mean. Of course, it depends on how I fall, in what manner I collapse. Supposing I fell off the bench while sitting there undisturbed, unprovoked, no wind or breeze to speak of, from a perfectly level position, that is, sitting quite erect on the bench placed on level ground, the book pulling me in neither one direction nor the other, just collapsing in on itself, flat on my lap, between my legs, which way would I go? I wonder. Straight ahead? Or straight ahead and a little to the left, or a little to the right? Or straight ahead and a lot to the left, or a lot to the right? Or maybe just to the left or just to the right, onto the bench rather than the ground? Obviously my train of thought has been stimulated by the present chapter, which he calls a book, or canto, I forget. Yet if I was in the room and shot from behind, standing there more or less in the middle of the room, it would be no laughing matter. For one thing, it would not be Mr Laurel doing the shooting, because it was he who lent me the book which I'm holding at the time and I'm sure he wouldn't want it to become soiled with blood from a gunshot wound, or possibly get the pages creased or perhaps even – as it fell to the ground with me desperately clutching it, as if it were something substantial like a piece of furniture or a low wall, which would be an odd item to have in the middle of a room, but then one's mind can play tricks under such circumstances – perhaps even, as I was saying, torn, since I do not realise what they are as I fall. Besides which he's been too nice to me, I think he's even made a pass at me, but I wouldn't want to bet my life on it because his facial expressions are somewhat erratic, peculiar to say the least, certainly not erotic, and one can never tell by looking at his face what he's thinking anyway. Not that he wears a poker faced expression. On the contrary, he's always smiling or frowning or crying or looking confused or distraught. But it's hard to tell when he's in love. Bergson, on the other hand, or literally on the settee or divan or sofa, I forget which, at any rate on the other side at some point, though not now, facing Mr Laurel, is a more likely suspect, and Mr Laurel is quite right to regard him with some suspicion while he's sitting and chatting with him. Bergson could easily come up from behind, through the open door between the two rooms, which is often kept open as Mr Hardy is somewhat insistent about knowing Mr Laurel's whereabouts, especially at night, and shoot me in the back from point-blank range. Moreover, he's just the type, if he were given to shooting, to shoot in the back. He knows very well that both Mr Hardy and Mr Laurel are at the moment feasting themselves at a benefit dinner for retired actors, since it was he who organised the event in the first place and personally invited the famous couple as honorary guests. Besides, his insanely jealous nature gives him away. I've seen his eyes turn spitefully cold and red or green whenever Mr Laurel has made an alleged pass at me. Frankly Mr Laurel doesn't know what he's doing half the time, though it must be precisely that which I find so sweet and cuddly in him that Bergson finds repugnant. I don't think Bergson thinks positively. So his only course of action, he decides, is murder; otherwise, he may feel, he would really become insane and possibly kill himself. Which is a much too negative and selfish way of thinking. But then he would think like that, if I know Bergson. And I do. Have I mentioned that he tried to seduce me once? Oh, it wasn't anything I couldn't handle, and it might have looked innocent enough to a casual observer, of which there were none, and it might even be said that I was misreading the signs, though believe me, I wasn't. It was just a light slap of his right hand on my left knee, or thereabouts, as I sat on a simple chair beside him and he sat on the chaise-longue, opposite Mr Laurel, who was seated behind his desk as usual, a slap that came down spontaneously, perhaps, with the last syllable of one of Mr Laurel's witticisms. I don't remember what the latter said, but the way the other's hand lingered just that extra fraction of a second, like when something funny has stopped being funny after everyone has offered a chuckle or a laugh, and when your smile wears thin and your laugh has become superfluous but your face needs just that extra fraction of a second to readjust itself to its former, presumably normal, expression – well, the way his hand lay on my thigh an instant longer than his smile on his face left no doubt in my mind as to his 'sense' of humour. His laughter didn't issue from the belly or the bowels, or even from the head for that matter, but from the groin, as if the comic, at least in my presence, had the same effect on him as an aphrodisiac. But there's something I neglected to mention. Namely, that being shot from behind I couldn't very well see who it was, I could only guess. After all, it could be Mr Hardy standing there, but that's another story involving another evening, since at the time Mr Hardy, along with Mr Laurel, is an honorary guest at a benefit dinner, as I've already said. Still, there's something else which puzzles me. It appears that the shot was fired from behind and from an ordinary pistol at point-blank range. (Don't ask me about model name and calibre, I know nothing about that sort of thing.) The question remains: was death instantaneous? You see, there's also the matter of the fractured skull caused by my fall, I believe, which still needs to be explained. It seems odd that I should fall backwards (the fracture's occurrence in the lower cranium, roughly equidistant from the ears, leads me to believe that I fell backwards) after having been shot in the back. I would have expected to fall forwards. And because it seems so odd I'm wondering whether to infer from this random fact that I was first struck with some deadly weapon on the back of the head and then, whilst falling either backwards or forwards (after all, I was discovered lying face down in the middle of the room), shot only a fraction of a second later, or even a few minutes later (who knows?). But if I pursue the matter too thoroughly and investigate every possible permutation I may never get back in time to straighten Mr Laurel's tie before he and Mr Hardy go out to their dinner party.

That's tomorrow. I forgot. A memory lapse. Was I thinking of something else, something more important? But if the dinner is only tomorrow, I'll continue. Though where was I? Fractured skull, wasn't it? Yes, it was, fractured. As to the question of the bullet, the gun, the who-fired-it and why, it's possible, after all, that someone used the butt of the gun to hammer my brains in (as in the movies) and, whilst doing so, inadvertently squeezed the trigger (though even in the movies such action is unlikely). For even if held by the barrel, which (if movies are anything to go by) is how a gun is handled when used as a club, it's still liable to go off unexpectedly, especially when one considers the complicated arrangement of the fingers holding it, for it could have been a case not of squeezing the trigger but rather of having it pushed by the knuckle of the index finger, or perhaps the middle finger, as a result of the thrust subsequent to, or simultaneous with, the blow on the head. In which case – and it seems that some of the evidence points to this hypothesis – the skin of the murderer's hand will have been scorched by the barrel as the gun went off, thereby removing any trace of fingerprints, while the bullet, purely by chance, will have passed cleanly through the heart, or the lungs, which is just as fatal. But surely the coroner would have mentioned that the angle of penetration indicates that the shot was fired from above (though they could never have established whether the gun was held by the handle or the barrel or in some other way) at about 45 degrees from the horizontal. Unless the police have asked the coroner to remain discreet about this detail so that they might set a trap for the murderer. The latter, acting on the assumption that the police suspect a cold-blooded gunman who shot his victim in the back at point-blank range, does everything possible to destroy any evidence that could lead to his being implicated in this sort of thing, namely cold-blooded murder. So he works up a sweat, tears his shirt to simulate a hot-blooded struggle, and dips his jacket in a filthy puddle. And when the time comes (as invariably it does in the movies) for our suspect to be arrested, he pulls out what he thinks is his trump card and submits boldly that he couldn't possibly have shot her cold-bloodedly from behind at point-blank range but that, as shown by the autopsy report (which he quotes verbatim without having seen it), he would have had to fire the gun upside-down from above at an angle of about 45 degrees from the horizontal while simultaneously inflicting a fatal blow to the back of her lovely cranium, which, he hypothesises, is how it must have happened and not, as the police version would have it, cold-bloodedly at point-blank range from behind. Naturally the police look chuffed, so pleased are they with their scheme, and point out to Mr Laurel (who, after all, may also be a suspect – we haven't discounted anyone yet) that only a bungling idiot would have done it that way and that he's a bungling idiot if they ever saw one. The police tend to be harsh and ill-mannered, and personally I don't believe a word of it; it sounds too much like a set-up. For one thing, Mr Laurel is too nice to me. He wouldn't even do it as a practical joke, although practical jokes are his stock in trade, in a sense. Mr Hardy, on the other hand, or strictly speaking in the other room, is another possible suspect. But then, for a start, that would involve a different evening from the one of the banquet, which means that Mr Laurel is at his desk as usual, for he hardly ever steps out without Mr Hardy, and surely he can see Mr Hardy coming in through the open door and tip-toeing up behind me. Why he gives no sign of warning is beyond me. Besides, if it's not the night of the banquet, I'm not there to straighten Mr Laurel's tie, as he's not used to wearing a black bow-tie, and when he does it's usually a clip-on job. Unless I'm there to borrow Mr Laurel's book, but then there's no reason for Mr Hardy to come into the room under any pretext whatsoever without knocking, silently turning the door-handle and tip-toeing up behind me, for the door is closed and Mr Laurel is at his desk, it being not the night of the banquet but a previous or subsequent night. For if Mr Laurel is there lending me the book, perhaps reading out selected passages for his amusement or my education, Mr Hardy would most certainly need some excuse to come into the room, he couldn't just walk in like that, door open or not, with the sole purpose of murdering me. Moreover, he has no motive, at least not as far as I'm aware. Admittedly I'm not all that familiar with Mr Hardy's motives, as he's rather reserved with women, perhaps even shy, and having never thought of myself as a mere sex object, let alone a murder victim, I do not consider myself qualified to judge him in this respect. Which brings me back to Bergson, who, besides having a warped sense of humour, might well be harbouring an incompetent fool beneath that suave, eloquent Gallic exterior. One never ceases to suspect. But as I'm only in the middle of Book Two I'd hate to come to any premature conclusion on the matter.

*

The writer said: It's all fiction, of course. He was trying to be rational and polite but anyone could see he was raving. As fictions go, he said, there's not a shred of evidence in it. Then he went on, trying to theorise his way out of a corner: The truth is either presumed at the outset or inferred at the conclusion. It's the x-factor around which the fiction revolves. But I'm not satisfied with it, this fiction, not satisfied at all. He was beginning to rave again. I'll tell you the truth. I'll tell it here and now. For all intents and purposes the story is over. No more stories. He sighed and took a deep breath.

I suffer. I suffer a great deal. Like everyone else, roughly. But my characters do not suffer. You've probably noticed this particularly un-human characteristic about them. Credibility or an equivalent term has sprung into your mind as you read. And what did you think? You've come this far, so the thought has probably crossed your mind, here and there, that things might change, that it won't go on this way forever. Let's wait and see, give it a chance, you said to yourself. Well, now it's over. This is the truth. Brace yourself, ..., he said, his tongue fishing for an epitaph. He was raving again, searching the expanse of language for a word that would mean 'voyeur' but without all that cinematic and foreign baggage attached to it. He considered the word 'observer' before opting against it. He considered, for the moment, not to consider any further alternatives but to stick with the simple and direct 'you'. He was showing signs of further raving before finally going on.

It all begins with a mood, or a colour, or the juxtaposition of a certain object with a certain feeling. And that is where it ends. Bergson, Mr Laurel and Mr Hardy are not inventions, yet not a syllable of truth has been uttered among them. Nor is L an invention. It is because I cannot remember her name and, consequently, must label her with an initial that she bears the semblance of an invention. I don't know what they are doing together, these people. I don't know who the narrator is. I don't know why the writer occasionally interferes; in fact, I often contradict him, sometimes without even knowing it. You will soon see why there's no point in going on.

*

It was in the middle of winter, or perhaps already spring, if an unusually cold spring. I was out for a walk. It was an ordinary day, perhaps a little cold for a spring day, if it was spring. The air was tranquil but unpredictable. When I saw her I didn't bother to check what she was reading. I was too far away at first, couldn't see the book, and besides, I was behind her. I didn't call out to her. I came up behind her, quietly enough. It was only after I stabbed her that I checked to see what she was reading. It couldn't have been my book in any case, since I was still writing it at the time, there was only the manuscript, one copy, it lay on the writing table, half written, half waiting to be written. Indeed it was precisely because it wasn't my book that I felt compelled to do it. And for the same reason there was no need to ascertain what she was reading; not by the wildest stretch of the imagination could it have been my book. I could not have been mistaken. It was a clean, brisk thrust between the ribs, the knife sinking up to the hilt as if she were made of butter. Which surprised me only a little. I hadn't practised at all, it seemed to come quite naturally to me. I think death was instantaneous. At any rate, she didn't move, she remained silent even, she didn't fall or lean one way or the other. I don't know who took the corpse to Mr Laurel's room. There is no Mr Laurel's room, and if there is it's empty, or someone else, completely unconnected with the affair, is now living there. Both Mr Laurel and Mr Hardy have been dead now for quite a few years. This is common knowledge. Their involvement seems totally incomprehensible and irrational to me. Likewise with Bergson. As for Virgil, he hasn't been seen on this planet, apart from one sighting of his ghost in the Swiss Alps, for over two thousand years. But I did go to Paris, though a long time ago, a different age and epoch. However, I did not expect to see Virgil there, and even if I did, I doubt that any Parisian could have told me where he was buried, let alone where he was living. Besides, Paris was different in his day, Lutetia Parisiorum, 'the mud-town of the Parisii', as it was called, and he never even set foot there. That was pure invention on my part. Only her hands showed any signs of violence, suddenly letting go of the book, fingers outstretched to their limits then freezing in a contorted and rather ugly gesture. I couldn't see her face. The book slid from her lap and fell to the ground: *The Georgics*, illustrated. It looked a hundred years old. Then I felt it all coming on, the confusion, the bickering characters, the search for motive, the plot thickening like French mud. Yet I managed to dispel it all easily enough, even the dreams. I must have felt guilty at some point. One dreams when one feels guilty.

Episode C: Abyssal Epistle

In the name of Verisimilitude, or an equivalent term, I say this, or this and that, or such and such and that but, or – for appearance's sake – in the middle of the journey of my life, but how would I know it is the middle, unless once the middle, unless the middle then, being now dead, being so, dead now and remembering, that's to say dead and yet remembering, if possible, if fathomable, unless the other way around, impossible that, then why dead go on, and how then such and such, how then interminably this or that, indefatigably such that, unremittingly going, insatiably on, unless unwittingly, dreamily, that's to say insensibly, in mid-trip, in April, or January, now August, end of bloom, in the name of Truth or an equivalent term. With regard to the story or novel or novella or long poem, or maybe merely lyric, epigram, haiku, couplet, line, or less, a word, sign, phoneme, brief pause, inconclusive pause, inconclusible breath, why dead go on, unless I say this such that, when all is said and done (not necessarily, but at least said), in February, such that this, by late September, or early October (at the latest) is that. I would say, Dear Mr Maro, hear this.

If you find it presumptuous of me to write like this and address you here, o say so and I'll shoot the writer and all his rebel characters. It's still common practice today. But – I'd open – would you be kind, no, gracious, no, patient – yes, perhaps patient – patient enough to hear a chapter, a short chapter, for my tongue is caught in mid-trill – hasn't it happened to you? – though the gods assure me it's only temporary, just part of the struggle, but I've stopped believing what they say, almost in fact stopped believing in the gods themselves, almost in fact stopped believing full stop because of the afflictions they bring upon me and my kind, so during hard times I'm forced to beg from people like you, to revert to a generalised faith in humanity. It is Decemberish dark and I have a vision without pretensions of surpassing the ending, though for now I wade through words because the mud from the rains of several millennia has started to dry and to crack, to cry mutely for a tear, which I can't offer. Would you – hope you don't find me impudent here – would you proffer a tear for my cause in your middle age, if only as a sign of acknowledgement, and perhaps append a little note, a summary, about this letter in the body of the tale, or if you like about some other chapter, an altogether different chapter, or about the whole of the story, if that's what we choose to call it, just a little note of approval or disapproval, a letter of reference to keep the thing alight (spiritually that is), even if it says you found the whole thing terrible, amateurish, in bad taste, even if it advises me to burn the lot, even if it's only a middling sort of response, noting how you liked some but not all, or all but not some, claiming reservations, doubts and second thoughts about this or that, or even if it's only of a technical nature, pointing out an excess or deficiency, say, of commas or semi-colons, or recommending a word here, not there, or there but not here, and even if it only says, yes, young man, get it published, submit it to my executors, Varius & Tucca, you'll find their address in the book (what book?) and I'll brief them about it in the meantime, though I can't promise they'll find you a publisher, they'll certainly try to help – sincerely, Publius Vergilius Maro; or under unhappier circumstances, a note regretting your inability to accede to my request due to ill health (yours, not mine, of course – mine would be no excuse); or under even more unhappier circumstances, a note asking me to desist from including its text in the body of the tale lest it contain some defamatory phrase or word or nuance (though I can't agree to that, Mr Maro, as a matter of principle: freedom of speech), though you may add a proviso such as for example: if you must print this crap at least take care to fictionalise proper names, as is only proper in these matters. Ah, I, would that I could! For there is indeed a fictional Virgil in the story, who is visited by the writer – isn't that fiction enough? Besides, to fictionalise your name and still uphold the name of Verisimilitude is beyond my artistic ingenuity, for the nearest fictional approximation to Maro is Mara, which unfortunately happens to be a name belonging to P, a dear friend who is as vulnerable to the onslaught of language as you or anyone else, even Mars, which, to my ears, is the next nearest approximation, but who would be equally offended by any libellous remark, whether referring to mortal or god, so that in striving to honour the name of Verisimilitude I'd be forced to amend Mars to Marx, which would mislead us into a treatise, so that Marx would have to be reduced to Mar, which on the face of it may sound OK, but if you think scripturally for a moment you'll recognise the word for 'bitter' in the Holy Tongue, to which a plethora of negative connotations is attached, not to mention secondary meanings in our own language; all of which would force me to continue my philological search and arrive at Ma, which obviously will not do, for on the one hand it produces an androgynous absurdity that may work successfully in some other genre, but not here, while on the other it calls to mind a refrain employed by a latter-day minstrel and would tempt me to write *Dear Ma, it's all right, I'm only dying* – which smacks of plagiarism and would undermine the credibility of my project; so that I'm stranded with a moribund M, which, I must confess, has a certain appeal and mystery about it. In fact I've used it before (so sincere was that appeal) – but then how could I use it in this letter to you and come out with my artistic integrity intact? I'm sure you'll agree, it would be a shameful act. Though the writer's personal prerogative for proper names is an inalienable right, surely there are limits that must not be transgressed. (I would be interested in your opinion on this matter.) Whereas a completely unrelated and fictitious name – say, Hollander – would invalidate the whole letter and render the story itself a travesty of fiction. For how could I expect you to reply to a letter addressed to Mr Hollander, and even if you did, on whose behalf would you be answering, your own or Mr Hollander's? There was a time, it was in March, I wrote to you under a different name and you answered in June and I read your little epistle in July; considerate as it was of you to answer, though you said nothing and will not now recognise the same person in that letter, it was also marked for the wrong person at the wrong time; for now it's like your May here, though we at opposite ends of the world call it November. What in the name of Verisimilitude, my dear Mario, am I to make of that? Sincerely, humbly and with ingratiating servility...

Episode D: A Banal Outcome

A note has slipped into the possession of the writer. It reads:

WRITER MURDERED L COMMA READER STOP
MOTIVE JEALOUSY OF NARRATOR STOP ACT OF
SPITE STOP WRITER CLAIMS MERCY KILLING
STOP LOYALTY STOP PITY STOP WANTED TO
SPARE HER ENDING STOP – NARRATOR

The writer wonders: will the narrative allow for Artur, infamous composer of ballads who, a century earlier, murdered the subjects of his ballads upon completion of his songs?

And in the park they said to one another, in the little square they said: I must revise, as if revisiting. I have new eyes, new marvels to fill there. I must trek the city, underground and overground, byways and boulevards. There is so little time sometimes. And sometimes so much of it. Shall I take the subway for pleasure or conveyance? Should I study the (averted) faces or merely note them in passing? I must rest in small gardens, parks, squares, a simple wooden bench will do. Perhaps I should occupy my time with a brief diversion whenever my feet are sore and hot, whenever the sensory input is excessive. I must undertake to translate abstract, quasi-geometrical shapes whenever there's a spare moment. I must have other pleasures, after all. One said don't go. One said I have a purpose. The former was obstinate. I must reconcile the two, don't you agree. I must visit the catacombs. They are simply marvellous. I cannot work in any other way. But you understand. Then to revisit, what warmer pleasure. And on each subsequent visit there is time for music, even rhetoric. I must listen, as I walk or sit, as if the sounds had meanings. I must learn to do that more easily, the way I learned to shop for bread, feigning not to touch the loaves but merely to pass my hand over them as in a blessing, yet fondling each one furtively, to test the crust. And what are the signs one said. Oh they are equivocal one said. I must forgive such dismissals, they belie their speakers. But they form a multitude whose voice is singular. And then I come to a side-street, a sort of alleyway, but immaculate, as if paved with sterilised linoleum, and witness a caress, a tiny impure gesture caught like a particle of dust in a beam of light. I must register the fact, however loathsome it may appear. I must remember to revise the guide of moral and aesthetic principles in the light of my experience. In the same light to compile the guides for experience and inexperience. This and more. To construct a dam for time. I must live with my commitments. I must remove my shoes, for a spell, while resting on the wooden bench. I must remember not to neglect the sun, to observe its position, lest I become lost. One said this is *The Georgics* do you know it. One said no pausing well I've heard of it. It is a charming book note the illustrations one said. Yes lovely a sort of treatise on farming isn't it one said. Yes and more filled with subtle wisdom one said. His large folio notebooks were full of epigrammatic verses which have not come down to us, while his epics were crammed into tiny pocket-size notebooks which have survived the centuries intact. Curious one said. Strange one said do you think there's some mystical significance in that. Such passing observations however shed neither light nor dark on the matter. But surely it is curious, is it not, that the reader, L, should be so motionless and unsuspecting, without intuition as it were, immediately prior to her violent death. One would have thought she'd see or hear something with her inner eye or ear. Or at the very least I could have provided a passer-by to warn her, perhaps with some discreet signal, a wink of the eye or a wave of the hand, of the impending danger. But this she cannot see if, as has been mentioned, she is engrossed in her book. Moreover, if she happens to look up, to rest her eyes on the contrasting landscape of the real world, she does so briefly, almost absent-mindedly, and if she happens to notice the signal, attaches to it a meaning too trivial to contemplate and consequently returns her gaze to the pages of the book without further ado. But she finds that she has lost her place. This could be the ultimate cause of her downfall. For had she heeded the signal she might have avoided her own death. But as I say, this is a matter of conjecture.

Alternatively, it is at an unsociable hour as they say, say 4 or 5 a.m., that she chooses to sit on the bench. In that case there is no-one to signal a warning. If it is late spring or early summer, it is dawn, and the birds in the nearby trees make a din which drowns out any sound the assailant might make, though, not being there, he does not make any. But surely at such an hour Bergson or Mr Laurel, or certainly Mr Hardy, who rightly or wrongly considers himself an intimate friend, would notice her absence and consequently raise the alarm. Besides, the light is coming from a source just above the horizon and at the latest, as has been remarked, it is early spring, which implies a social hour, say 8 or 9 a.m., or possibly the afternoon. A passer-by is nearby. Perhaps she hasn't noticed him. (It is only after the event that one can say, more or less objectively, what really happened, if one happened to be at the scene of the crime, unperceived by anyone.)

One enters the park, or square (strictly speaking, if it is a square, it is so only by name, its dimensions outlining a shape partly polygonal, partly circular), through an open gate at one of the many corners, some of which coincide with street-corners, others with the back-yards of Victorian houses. An air of déjà vu surprises one at some point in the week. One comes here often enough, no doubt, but the exact positions of human, animal and vegetable life are fixed only to a given moment in time, so that an exact recurrence or duplication of the scene conjures up eerie associations in the most unsuspecting mind. A man in a grey suit has just appeared and is about to step onto a small corner of grass in order to cut short the distance between the pavement he is on and the one that meets it an angle a little further ahead. He is walking in one's direction, away from a female figure seated in the middle of a plain bench, apparently reading, her back facing obliquely towards the other's. A small cluster of trees is in mid-bloom. A few birds are heard from that direction. Two birds can be seen on separate branches of the nearest tree. A dog is seen trotting in on the left towards the space between the man and the woman, cutting their line diagonally. Its owner cannot be seen, but his or her person can be assumed to be somewhere nearby, perhaps behind.

You are not from these parts, I presume. Why should you presume anything, I come here every day except when the weather is intolerable and prevents me from doing so. Now that is a piece of curiosity, for it's the same with me, though I only pass through, I never sit down, but I have never seen you here before. Then you are either extremely myopic or a little deceitful. I assure you I'm neither, at the worst a little hard of hearing sometimes, it's the traffic, overexposure the doctors call it, my room overlooks a very busy street, but that shouldn't affect my noticing you here. My name is L, do take a seat. No, I really must be on my way, I never sit here, but thanks just the same. You are presuming again, it

was mere cordiality on my part, this is *The Georgics*, do you
know it? No, but I hope I shall, perhaps under more
congenial circumstances. The exchange does not take place.
Instead, several pigeons are visible from
several directions, though
not from a great distance,
perched on a central spire
on a protuberance or relief of sorts
in a circle just below the peak,
from a great distance blending with the stone
and, as at night, however close, invisible,
at all other hours in positions
largely immaterial to the time of day, gurgling
to themselves one must suppose, or musing
absently above around and within the fount,
flitting to any of the four smaller spires
that loom between circumference and middle,
or alighting on the dry basins or when filled on the rims,
or nearer the ground, on one of the three concrete steps
of each of eight surrounding approaches,
or even comically under the chin of the colonel's bust
set in relief in the side of a smaller spire,
or on his nose, enough to make you sneeze,

enough to make you roll in fits
on the octagonal base of cobblestone. 3:15,
partly sunny, spring, March or April,
coming down the northerly walk
through dappled shade
or dappled sunlight
the fountain's shadow up ahead in the open square-like space
gaining to the left,
the sun presumably setting to the right,
falling (the shadow that is) over two three concrete steps
one-eighth the octagonal base,
strictly speaking it must be north-northwest or due
northwest, the path,
for the shadow to fall that way
squarely on the eighth part of the base
aligned with the edge of the square steps
which have no shadows
to speak of
being for the moment submerged
in a greater shadow –
not silence, under no condition
am I speaking of silence
when I say shadow,

not that there isn't any silence
to speak of –
then, after the steps,
running onto the cobblestone relic,
preserved in the shape of an octagon
what might once have been a shapeless expanse
or perhaps nevertheless an octagon by origin,
amid a field of concrete and asphalt
bordered by park grass and further away
trees, the usual assortment,
nor is the space of concrete and asphalt
between fountain and grass and further away
the usual assortment of trees
undefined,
but forms a thick-set cross
like the red cross
only grey
upon which the occasional pigeon
will alight, then totter. From this distance you don't suspect
a cobblestone surround in the middle of asphalt ground, it
comes as a mild surprise. But the shadow is drawn from
inference as you walk down through the dappled shadows
gaining leftward or the dappled sunlight waning on the

right, from the northwest, under your feet as it were. It follows that all shadows run parallel, in a way, and as you get nearer you see this is so, somehow, but the real surprise as you get near enough is the cobblestone octagon and the way the whole, after brief circumspection of the scene, is inlaid in a subtle cross as if the pigeons perched in nooks and crevices, on pinnacles and steps, were by extension one with sunlight or shadow falling on the leaves of trees at the park's perimeter, or beyond, in the remote depths of the city in general, though this in fact may only be conjecture.

—London, 1980-1995

GAD HOLLANDER's books are: *Walserian Waltzes* (Avec Books, Penngrove, CA 2000), *The Palaver* (Book Works, London 1998), with visual work by Andrew Bick, *Sleep, Memory* (New Pyramid Press, London 1988) and *Figures of Speech* (edition fundamental, Cologne 1987). His work has appeared in the literary journals *Curtains*, *Central Park*, *Acts*, *Temblor*, *Reality Studios*, *Paper Air*, *First Intensity* and *untitled*. He has also directed the films/videos *The Palaver Transcription* (2000), *Diary of a Sane Man* (1990), shown at the Berlin Film Festival & broadcast on Channel 4 (UK); *Euripides' Movies* (1987); *Background Music (Orphic)* (1986) and *Mnemosyne* (1985). He lives in London, was born in Jerusalem and spent (in/un-) formative years in Queens, New York.

Other Pivotal Prose Titles: